I am Just Me,
HEAR ME ROAR!

Written by Cara L. Coleman
Illustrated by Lori Schue

Copyright © 2010 by Cara L. Coleman. 73035-COLE

Library of Congress Control Number: 2010906927

ISBN:
Softcover   978-1-4535-0080-4
Hardcover 978-1-4535-0081-1

This book was printed in the United States of America.

To order additional copies of this book, contact:
Xlibris Corporation
1-888-795-4274
www.Xlibris.com
Orders@Xlibris.com

DEDICATION:

For J-Cole, G-money man, Hopey-J and Ziah Trina: I love you big, big, big, soopty dooper hoopty mooper alley looper much… and little bit.- Mama love

MUCHAS GRACIAS:

To the Virginia Board for People with Disabilities and the Partners in Policymaking Program: Thank you for providing me the opportunity for a true (and FREE) edu-macation.

To GG, Papa T, G-Ma and Papa Homer: Thank you for the love and the logistics- you made it all possible.

To Kathie Snow, most honored PIP graduate and revered mentor: Thank you for the words and for helping me set Justice's voice free.

To the "uptight" artist next door (who has the king of curmudgeon's for a husband): Thank you for believing in me, drawing hope and loving my be-bes!

For more info and great advocacy, check out:

www.disabilityisnatural.com

www.partnersinpolicymaking.com

www.vaboard.org

My name is Justice Hope Coleman
and I am 4 years old.

I am a little sister, a big sister,

a daughter, a granddaughter, a great granddaughter,

a niece, a cousin and a friend.

I have a puppy named Minuit and my
family has a dog named Sadie.
Minuit is as shiny and black as midnight.
Her fur is so thick and soft that I wish
I could disappear in it.
Sadie has a big, very loud bark.
She sounds mean. She won't do anything
but wag her tail and lick your face off.

I am in preschool.

I ride the big yellow bus to school.

I love my teachers. They make me smile.

We read together and

play with all kinds of toys.

I love to have art class.

We have circle time everyday.

My mom meets me when I get

off the bus after school.

I am so happy to see her.

I think she is happy to see me

because she gives me big hugs and kisses.

We like to stretch out and talk about my day.

Then we eat lunch together.

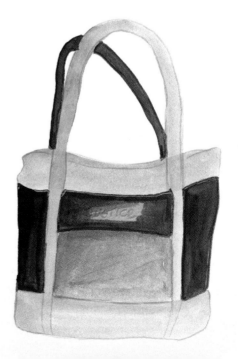

I love to play with my big brother, Gibraltar,

and my baby sister, Kezziah.

Gibraltar and I love to wrestle.

I am not as strong as he is,

so he is gentle with me.

Kezziah doesn't wrestle with us yet.

She is too little.

Kezziah lies on her play mat and watches us.

She squeals and laughs.

We start laughing too.

Gibraltar tickles her and then he tickles me.

We laugh more.

I get so excited.

I get louder and louder.

I can't hold it in.

I ROAR with laughter.

Gibraltar jumps up and

runs around the room roaring.

I can get up and move around the room too.

My mom picks me up and

helps me into my wheelchair.

I roar like a tiger.

Gibraltar growls like a cheetah.

Kezziah tries hard to turn her laugh into a roar.

Her voice is still too new.

She squeaks and meows like a baby tiger cub.

Gibraltar pushes me in my wheelchair.

I have to keep my roar quiet

as we creep around the corner,

hiding in the savannah

in the wild of Africa.

We are hunting Zebra.

We get very close to the Zebra

drinking from the watering hole.

Suddenly, they smell us and stop.

We pounce.

Cheetah King Gibraltar and

Tiger Queen Justice

chasing Zebras.

I have a disAbility.

It does not make me a scary monster.

I am not sick.

You can't catch a disAbility like you catch a cold.

I am not broken.

I don't need to be fixed.

There is nothing wrong with me.

My disAbility is natural.

I am a kid just like you.

My disAbility just means I move differently.

I am able to use a wheelchair to play tag,

Duck, Duck, Goose

and kick a ball around.

My disAbility just means I talk differently.

I talk all the time, often very loudly, and

I have a lot to say. (Ask my mom.)

I just express myself in my own way.

I am able to use my eyes and

an apparatus that looks like a big button

to help me communicate.

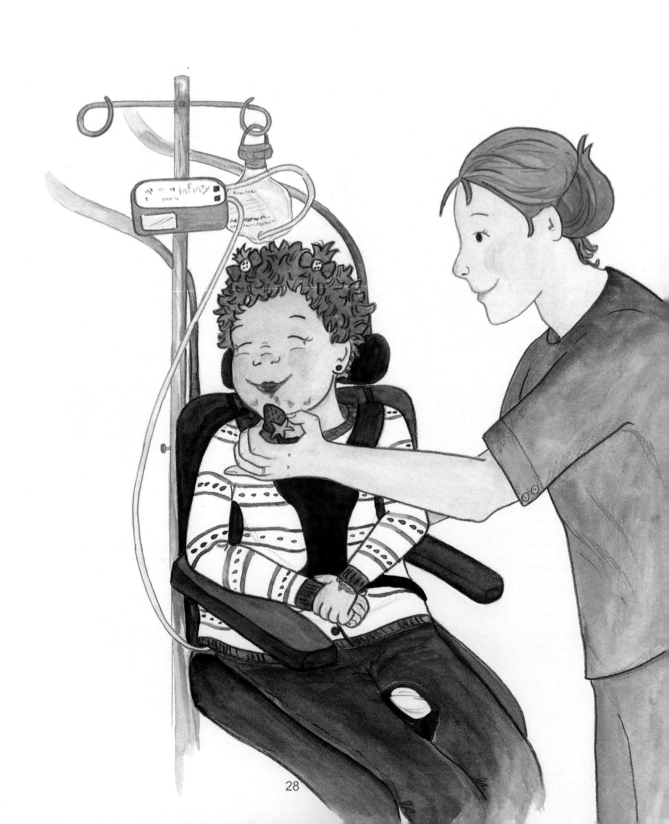

My disAbility just means I eat differently.
A pump machine helps put food
into my stomach.
I am also able to taste things.
My favorite foods are strawberries
and my friend Ms. Mayra's
homemade spaghetti sauce.

My disAbility just means I see differently.

I am able to see better out of the side of my eyes.

So, I move my head around to find you

or to see my toys.

Sometimes I wear glasses.

Gibraltar does all of these things in a different way than you and me. Kezziah even does all of these things in her own way too. Everyone in the world has differences. Each of us is unique.

FOR I, THE LORD LOVE JUSTICE

But did you know I am
more like you than
I am different from you?

I really like dolls
and stuffed animals.

I adore red, anything
shiny and sparkly,
and dressing up.

I love books and
reading.

I am always listening to, dancing to

and making music.

Swimming is my favorite sport.

I could float back and forth

on the swing all day long.

I love how the wind

tickles my face when

I sit back in my stroller

and take my puppy for a walk.

I am a kid.

Just like you.

I have feelings just like you too.

I love it when you say "Hi" to me.

It hurts me when someone stares

or points at me and doesn't

want to be my friend.

I need my mom and dad to hug me

when I am hurt.

I am not always happy

when I have to go to bed early

or take a bath

(especially when my mom

scrubs my face or ears.)

I feel proud when I sing a song

in circle time

and everyone claps for me.

I feel awful when someone

laughs at how I sing.

Sometimes I share all of my secrets,

thoughts, and feelings with

my companion dog, Minuit.

She doesn't laugh at me.

She listens, snuggles in

and dreams along with me.

Other times,

I don't even have to say anything,

she knows what I am thinking or feeling

and she lays her head across my lap.

I feel pretty when I put on

a new dress for a party.

I feel sad when the party ends

and I have to go home.

I am a kid.

Just like you.

So do you want to come to our house

today and play in the wild?

I'll tell my mom you are coming.

How fast are you?

I can move fast in my wheelchair.

You can push me.

Do you want to go to the watering hole?

Or climb a mountain?

My big brother and little sister

will play with us too.

What animal do you want to be?

I will be the tiger.

I am Justice.

Hear me ROAR!

DISCUSSION GUIDE:

A kid's Interview with Justice and her mommy

It is always okay to ask questions so you will learn about Justice and can become her friend.

What "happened" to Justice? Why doesn't she do things the way I do them? Just as you were born to look, think, and move the way that you do, Justice was born to look, think and move the way that she does. Her differences are natural just like being born with red hair or having big feet. Look around at all of the different people in the world and you will see that none of us are exactly alike, even twins are different in some ways. Thankfully all of our differences don't interfere with us being friends and having fun.

How do you know what Justice is saying? I look at her eyes and her face to tell me. If she is looking at something specific, like a doll or a book, she is pointing at it. If she is looking at me, she is speaking to me. She smiles when she is happy and frowns when she is sad. I look at her body- her arms, her hands, her head, or her chest to tell me what she is saying. Justice moves her arms and shakes her head when she is excited. She cries when she is unhappy or uncomfortable. I look at what is going on around us: like what time it is, where we are, who is around us and what we are doing. Justice can also speak to you using a device called a "switch." It is a big button that Justice pushes to speak with you. Justice works hard to communicate. Together, we can piece together all of the forms and methods of expression to figure out what Justice is saying.

How do I know that Justice knows me? Justice may open her eyes wide and raise her eyebrows when she hears you. She may move her head to see or hear you better. Sometimes when she is listening to you, she grows very still and silent- so you know you have her attention. She will also make sounds to communicate with you. Justice may smile, shake her body, giggle and shout or roar (a happy shout/roar) when she knows you and is happy to see you. Sometimes she makes very specific noises that sound like letters in response to something you just asked or said to her.

How do I talk to Justice? Talk to her like you talk to your brothers, sisters and other friends: with your voice, your heart and your hands. Justice hears everything you say and do. She loves to listen to you talk. While Justice may communicate with you in a different way, she wants you to talk to her in the same way you talk to others.

Can Justice walk? Justice does not walk right now. She is working on teaching her legs to help her stand. Justice uses something called a "stander" to help get her body upright. She lays on the stander and once she is buckled in, we raise her up. Justice loves to show off how she is tall like her daddy. She has a desk on the stander for school work, games and crafts. The stander has wheels so she can move around in it. She hopes to learn to walk someday. In the meantime, she uses a wheelchair to get around everywhere. What could be greater than being chauffeured everywhere in a comfy chair with big, fast wheels?

How do I play with Justice? Grab a toy, a book, or some paint and paper and play with Justice just like you do with your brothers, sisters and other friends. Justice likes to play, just like you. Justice loves balls, music and finger paint. As you get to know Justice and play with her, you'll figure out how Justice may do things differently. It'll be fun! She can play catch by rolling the ball back and forth or by pushing the ball off her desk to you. She can play soccer using the front wheels of her wheelchair to kick. Justice can listen, sing and dance to music if you push her around in her wheelchair to the beat. If you tape some paper to the desk of her stander and squirt some paint onto it, Justice will paint with her fingers, arms and elbows.

But do I have to be extra careful when I play with Justice? What if I hurt her when we are playing? Justice is tough but she can get hurt just like you if playing gets too rough. She would rather have you play with her and not worry that she will break because she won't.

Why doesn't Justice eat like me? Justice's mouth just works a bit differently than yours. When you eat, you chew your food, swallow it, and then it goes down your throat to your tummy. Justice has difficulty chewing and swallowing, so we are able to put the food right into her tummy. She can taste food- the best part of eating- but she doesn't have to do all that chewing! Justice likes to taste foods on her lips or tongue.

How does the food get into Justice's stomach? There is a small button on her tummy. The button is connected to a little straw inside her tummy. We connect a tube to her button and the feeding pump puts the liquid through the tube into the straw right inside her tummy.

Expand

your vocabulary with words that are important to

Justice Hope Coleman

Ability: noun, (ah- bil-eh-tee) A natural or acquired skill or talent.

Accessible: adjective, (ak-ses-uh-buhl) Can be reached, used (like a playground or swing), entered (like a door or building), etc. by all people; obtainable or attainable.

Adapt: verb, (uh-dapt) To adjust or modify to fit different needs, requirements, environments or conditions; to change something, like a toy, so that it can be used by all people.

Apparatus: noun, (ap-uh-rat-us) Instruments, machinery, tools or materials that have a particular function or are intended for a specific use; any complex instrument.

Communicate: verb, (kah-myoon-eh-cate) To convey or reveal information, to make known, to show.

Companion: noun, (kuhm-pan-yuhn) Partner, friend, confidante, accomplice, pal, playmate, guide, protector, sidekick, ally, crony, comrade, and buddy.

Difference: noun, (dif-er-unce) A distinguishing characteristic; distinctive quality, feature, etc.

DisAbility: noun, (dis-ah-bil-eh-tee) Different skills or talents or a body part that works differently; for example: different way of moving or different way of communicating.

Express: verb, (x-spress) To share feelings or opinions; to set forth in words, symbols, gestures, statements, art.

Gibraltar: noun, (ja-bral-ter) This is the name of Justice's big brother and also means an invincible fortress or stronghold. A British colony at the northwest end of the Rock of Gibraltar, a peninsula on the south-central coast of Spain in the Strait of Gibraltar, connecting the Mediterranean Sea and the Atlantic Ocean between Spain and northern Africa.

Hope: noun, (hohp) Justice's middle name and a belief or feeling that what is wanted, desired or dreamed of can be achieved or had; belief or feeling that an event or circumstance will turn out for the best.

Justice: noun, (jus-tis) Virtue, fairness, equality and righteousness. The quality of being just; moral rightness; conformity to moral rightness in action or attitude.

Kezziah: noun, (ku-zy-yuh) The name of Justice's little sister; a Hebrew word for cinnamon. From the Old Testament, the name of Job's second daughter born after his sufferings (see Job 42:14). The name has been taken to symbolize female equality, since all of Job's three daughters received an inheritance from their father, an unusual circumstance in a time period when women and men were not treated equally.

Minuit: noun, (min-wee) This is the name of Justice's puppy pal; it is French and means midnight. Midnight is not only completely black, but it is the time when one day ends and a new one begins.

Natural: noun, (nah-chur-el) Present or produced in nature, inherent, essential characteristic, not acquired.

Savannah: noun, (sa-vahn-uh) One of the places Justice and her siblings like to pretend to play; It is the cross between a grassland and desert; forty percent of the wildlife are mammals, such as the lion, zebra, giraffe, tiger, baboons, elephant, rhinoceros, and gazelle; also are amphibians and hundreds of bird species; many of the animals have adapted to the climate, such as the cheetah, who developed the ability to pursue their prey at high speeds.

Stander: noun, (staahn-dur) This is the piece of equipment Justice uses to help her stand; equipment that helps a person whose legs work differently stand upright and move around to participate in different activities.

Switch: noun, (swich) This is the device Justice and others who talk differently can use (by pushing a button) to speak, read, or sing pre-recorded words; formally known as an "alternative augmentative communication" device.

Unique: adjective, (you-neek) Only one of its kind; without an equal or equivalent.

Watering Hole: noun, Tiger queen Justice and Cheetah King Gibraltar hunt here; a place in Africa where animals gather to drink water.

Wheelchair: noun, (wee-uhl-chair) A chair on wheels that is used by a person who moves differently to access her/ his world.

Justice's Bubble Wrap Fun

In the story, Justice shows you how much she likes to create art. One way to create interesting art is by using unusual materials such as plastic bubble wrap. Justice likes to feel the texture of the bubble wrap and paint and creates awesome prints.

Materials:

Paper, Tempera Paints, Bubble Wrap, Rollers or Brushes, Newspaper and a Tray or Cookie Sheet

1. Place the bubble wrap onto newspaper for easy clean up. Squeeze paints into a tray or cookie sheet.
2. Use a roller or brush to paint over the bubble wrap. You can even use your hands if you like.
3. Place clean paper over the bubble wrap and press gently.
4. Lift up to see the bubble wrap print!

To create a bubble wrap bee hive:
1. Use gold or yellow paint to make a bubble wrap print on black or brown paper.
2. To make the bee bodies, dip your thumb in orange paint and press it down on the hive.
3. Dip your finger tip in white paint and give it two wings.

After you have made your bubble wrap art, tell someone how you printed with bubbles!

Justice's Finger Paint Art

In the story, Justice shows you how she likes to finger paint. When you finger paint you can use the motion of your hands to create art called action painting. Sometimes she pretends she is in the ocean and creates action art of the waves with her finger paint.

Materials:

Paper and Tempera or Finger Paints

1. Place paper onto newspaper for easy clean up.
2. Squeeze paint onto the paper and use your hands to move it around. Think about being in the ocean water and how the water sways with the waves. Use your hands to move the paint over the paper.

To create an octopus in your ocean:

1. Let your finger painted ocean dry.
2. Spread different color paint onto the palm side of your hand using a roller or brush or simply by pressing your hand into paint.
3. Now make a handprint on your dry ocean painting. Turn the painting so the legs of your octopus hang down.
4. Give your octopus 2 eyes. Dip your thumb into different color paint and print 2 thumb print eyes on the head.

After you have made your finger paint ocean, tell someone how you created the ocean water and the octopus.

Be creative like Justice!

"I am Justice, Hear Me Roar" Art Activities were created especially for this story by Artlingz, Inc. ™

Visit www.artlingz.com or www.seesaycreate.com to learn how
you can share your artwork with your friends.

These activities were modified from Artlingz Adaptive Art Activities titled
Bubble Wrap Art and Finger Paint Ocean.

Artlingz Adaptive Art activities are especially intended for exploring many ways of creating art.

Visit www.artlingz.com for more art activities that include facts, art vocabulary,

easy steps, helpful hints and exciting ideas for creating art every day.

Adaptive Art™ is a division of Artlingz, Inc™

dedicated to helping all artists find ways to express themselves.

This SeeSayCreate™ book combines literature and art activities for
a whole minded creative approach to learning. See the story, Say the words, Create awesome art!
All art projects were developed especially for this book by Artlingz, Inc. ™, an online creativity warehouse
of fun and educational art activities for everyone.
Look for more SeeSayCreate™ books for budding readers and artists.
Visit www.seesaycreate.com today!

See SayCreate™
Stories for Creative Minds

Have more fun doing art! Visit www.artlingz.com today!

Edwards Brothers Malloy
Thorofare, NJ USA
May 9, 2012